Grub in Love

For Dave with love—A.B.

For Lee—S.W.

little bee books

An imprint of Bonnier Publishing Group
853 Broadway, New York, New York 10003
Text copyright © 2010 by Abi Burlingham.
Illustrations copyright © 2010 by Sarah Warburton.
First published in Great Britain by Piccadilly Press.
This little bee books edition, 2015.
LITTLE BEE BOOKS is a trademark of Bonnier Publishing Group,
and associated colophon is a trademark of Bonnier Publishing Group.
Manufactured in China 0240815
First Edition 2 4 6 8 10 9 7 5 3 1
Library of Congress Control Number: 2015934178
ISBN 978-1-4998-0134-7

www.littlebeebooks.com
www.bonnierpublishing.com

Grub
in Love

by Abi Burlingham
illustrated by Sarah Warburton

little bee books

This is me.

I'm Ruby.

This is Grub.

He's a grubby, messy pup!

He's always getting into trouble.

But this time—

you won't believe what he did!

Some new people moved in next door.

There's a boy named Billy.

I'm not very happy about that.

I don't like boys.

There's also a dog named Tilly.

Grub's not very happy about that.

Grub crouches by the fence
and growls and won't move an inch.
He shakes his head at the flowers.
He shakes his head at the fence.
He is definitely not happy.

One day, I moved a plank and peeked through the fence.

Billy and Tilly were playing soccer.

It looked like lots of fun.

I wished I could play with them.

Grub just growled.

Then, guess what happened?

Billy kicked the ball right over **our** fence.

Do you know what Grub did?
He chased it,
he kicked it,
he headed it,
and he rolled right over it.

Billy peeked through his side of the fence
and laughed and laughed.
Billy seemed like he'd be fun to play with.
Maybe he wouldn't be so bad,
even though he is a boy.
I wished Grub liked Tilly.
But he just growled.

Then, after the first day,
and the second day,
and the third day,
and the fourth day,
Grub stopped growling.
Do you know why?

He was peeping at Tilly through the fence . . .

. . . and Tilly was peeping at Grub.

Then the trouble really started.

Grub moaned and groaned.

He grunted and grumbled.

He snorted and sniffed.

I said, "Dig, Grub, dig."

But Grub wouldn't dig.

Do you know what he did?

He hung his head,

and his ears went flip flop.

At night he made this crying noise.

Mom covered her ears.

Dad covered his ears.

I covered my ears.

Joe covered his eyes—

I have no idea why.

Mom said, "Grub's in love. He's pining."
It sounded more like whining to me.

Joe's too little to understand.
He thinks Grub has a cold.

He sat in Grub's bed and patted his head.
"Poor Gub," he said.

In the morning,

Grub wouldn't eat his food.

He just stared at it.

Then he stared at me.

Then I scratched his floppy ears.

That cheered him up a bit!

Billy said Tilly was the same way.
Billy said she would only eat cheese
and crusty bread.
I think Tilly might be French.

We bought Grub a toy bird to cheer him up.

"Look, Grub, look!" I said.

"You'll love her.

She's got a squeak."

But Grub didn't love her at all,

not one bit.

I think Mom is right. Grub loves Tilly.

The next day, Grub started digging again—
under the fence!
Do you know what Tilly did?
She started digging too!
I pulled and pulled to get Grub back.
Billy pulled and pulled to get Tilly back.
Then they both started whining.
"I've had enough!" said Mom.

So Billy and I had a meeting by the fence.

It was very important.

We talked about Grub and Tilly.

Then we each had a lemonade-flavored popsicle

and hunted for snails.

I collected them in a bucket.

We had nine!

It was very nice.

But we still didn't know what to do about

Grub and Tilly.

That night,
Grub scratched and scratched and scratched
at the back door
and made all the paint come off.
It looked like such a mess.
"That's it!" said Mom. "I really have had enough."

So the next day my mom and Billy's mom
and me and Billy
decided to have a picnic,
all of us together—
with Grub and Tilly!

It was the best picnic ever!
We had bread and cheese and
strawberry tarts,
and we played soccer.

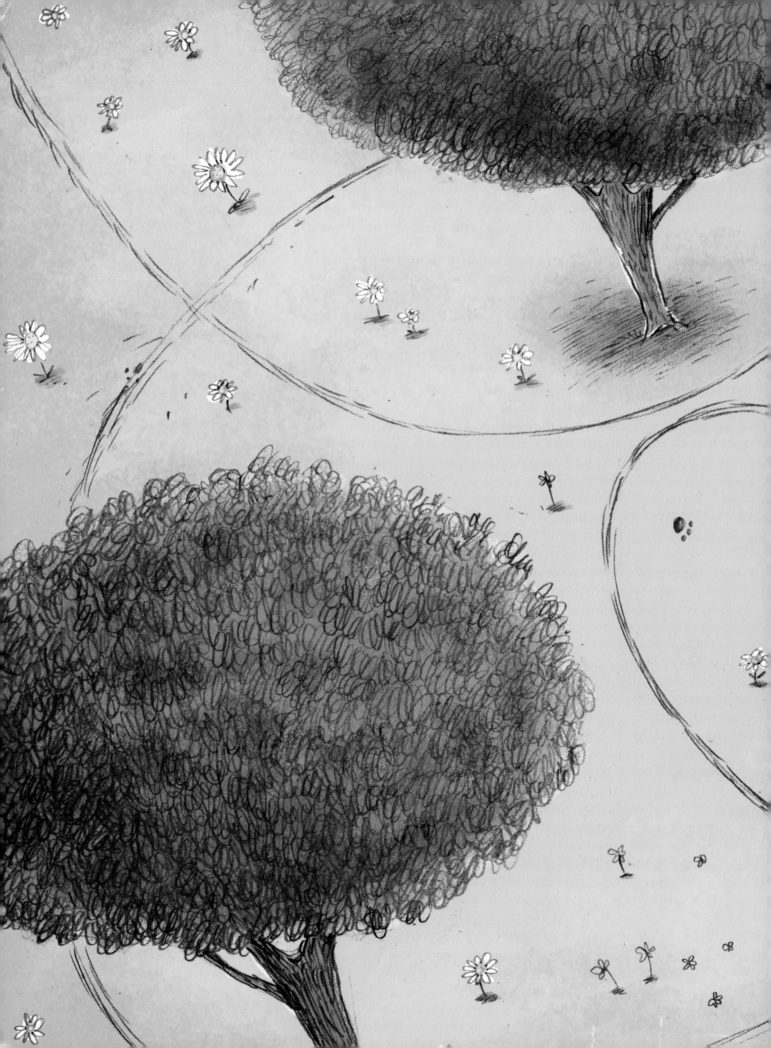

Do you know what Grub and Tilly did?

They raced around the trees,

they chased each other's tails,

and they ran so far that we had to go and look for them.

When we found them,

Grub's tail was wagging the most I've ever seen.

In the morning, Grub ate all his food.

"Good dog, Gub!" said Joe.

Then Grub dug three holes
in the garden.

"Bad dog, Gub!" said Joe.

But it wasn't bad, really.

It was good . . .

because a digging Grub
was a happy Grub.

"Would you like to have another picnic
with Tilly?" I asked Grub.
Do you know what Grub did?

He gave me the
BIGGEST, messiest hug
ever!